A NOTE FROM THE AUTHOR

While living in Istanbul in 2008, I saw a feral parrot just like Mustafa perched on a tall fir tree not far from our balcony in Üsküdar, Istanbul, Turkey. I was surprised and began to imagine what its life was like living in this huge metropolis. All the people and animals in the book are named after students and friends that I have meet in Istanbul.

While the idea of a book was mine, I knew I needed to find an illustrator from somewhere in Turkey. A friend encouraged me to ask a local high school art department if I could run a competition. Through that I was led to Joy Perdue, who has done a wonderful job capturing the sites of Istanbul for this children's book.

May you enjoy the journey, and realize that being found is the cry of every heart.

Lost in Istanbul

Written by Carla Petersen

Illustrated by Joy Perdue

ISBN-10: 151515985X

ISBN-13: 978-1515159858

DEDICATION

My heart goes out to the many whom I have met and befriended not only in Istanbul, but also all throughout the beautiful country of Turkey. I found myself in Turkey and discovered His great plan for me. —- Carla

My life has taken many twists and turns but I would like to dedicate this book to my mom. She is a great catalyst and encourager in my life. I am blessed to be her daughter. —- Joy

Written by Carla Petersen

Illustrated by Joy Perdue

Meet Zehra.

She lives in Istanbul, a large city crossing two continents.

If we go to her house, we will meet her father, mother, brother and cat, Ramazan.

Zehra’s biggest fear is getting lost.

N
W
E
S
Istanbul
KAĞITHANE
BEŞIKTAŞ
ŞIŞLI
EYÜP
BEYOĞLU
FATIH
ÜSKÜDAR
EMIÖNÜ
Çay

PET SHOP

One day in the market, Zehra stopped to look at a beautiful green toy. She wound it up, and it made squawking noises. She smiled.

A few minutes later, Zehra looked up and couldn't see her mother anymore. She was scared. She felt lost. But as quickly as the fear came it left when she heard her mother's voice calling, "Zehra, Zehra, what are you doing?"

Mother started to scold Zehra, but when she saw the tears in Zehra's eyes, she grabbed her tightly saying, "Don't ever do that again! Do you hear me?" Her mother's hug warmed her inside from the top of her head to the tip of her toes.

"What do we have here?" asked her mother. Zehra tenderly released the toy parrot into her mother's hands. "Ah, I see. Do you like this one? Let me show you a surprise. Come with me!"

They pulled their purchases behind them over cobble stone streets and through the crowd.

Arriving at a small shop not far from the central fountain, they were greeted by all kinds of creatures. There in the center of the shop sat the most beautiful bird Zehra had ever seen!

A big green parrot with a bright orange beak! It was just like the one she had held at the market. His name was Mustafa.

“Mom can I have him? Can we take him home? Please, Mom, please?!?”

“No Zehra, but we can come and visit. It will be our special time together each week. We need to go home now and get ready for our relatives.”

Zehra gently nodded, thinking to herself, *I almost got lost but instead I got to see one of the most beautiful birds in the world! Today I am the luckiest girl in all of Istanbul!*

PET SHOP
CAT FOOD
CAT FOOD
DOG FOOD
DOG FOOD
FOR SALE
HAMSTERS

So every Saturday for a month, Zehra and her mother had the same routine. They went to the market and then visited the pet store.

Then one Saturday there was no parrot! The shopkeeper said that he sold it to a man just a few hours earlier.

Zehra was very sad and just wanted to go home.

But when they arrived home

...there was a present waiting for Zehra!

Today she was six years old and the big gift on the table was for her!! Her father encouraged her to unwrap it quickly while Murat, her younger brother, kept jumping up and down. “Hurry, Hurry! Open it!” he shouted.

Under the cover was none other than the beautiful green parrot, Mustafa! He was now her very own! The cage was taken upstairs and placed on a table in the middle of Zehra's room. "Now you will have to feed him and take care of him. He is your responsibility, Zehra," her father said. "Happy Birthday!"

Life for Mustafa was never dull. Ramazan liked to climb up on the table and tease the parrot. Murat was often in Zehra's room causing trouble. But Zehra loved to have Mustafa fly around her room and make his squawking noises.

One night, a few weeks before school started, Zehra's mom helped her learn her address so she wouldn't get lost. "Repeat after me, 429 Lale Sokak, Üsküdar."

They did this for a week, every night at bedtime: the repeating of her address, kissing her Mom goodnight and wishing sweet dreams to Mustafa.

And every night, Mustafa would sit on his perch, under his cover and wish he could be free.

This cage is such a small place,

A small space to live.

Every night dreams of beautiful flights,

Beautiful sights fill my head.

When can I go?

When can I fly?

When can it be my turn to try?

A few days before school started, a most awful thing happened. Zehra was in her room getting ready, and heard her mom calling from the kitchen, “Breakfast!” Zehra ran down the stairs, shouting, “Coming, Mom!”

After Zehra left, Murat tip-toed in and opened the cage to play with the parrot, not realizing the window was open. Murat giggled as Mustafa flew around and around the room.

Then with one swoosh of his wings…

Mustafa flew right out the window!

Murat cried out but Mustafa was free, circling higher and higher until at last he landed on a tall tree.

The world is such a big place,

A big space to be.

This day is filled with beautiful flights,

Beautiful sights for me to see.

Where can I go?

Where can I fly?

All at once it is my turn to try!

“I’m free! I want to see it all! I want to go everywhere!”

A black crow greeted him, “You want to experience the world? Come with me! I’ll take you on the ride of your life!”

Off they went, dipping and turning, dodging and spinning into the beautiful world of the open waters. “This way, follow the boats, man! You want to see more of the world? Follow the boats into the dock and head up to that tall building — Taksim! The pigeons can direct you. I’ve got business to do. Tell ‘em Ali sent you!”

The pigeons took Mustafa one last swoop over the hill and Taksim Square was before them.

Then he heard a young child scream, “Look, Mom! A parrot! I know I can catch it!” Before Mustafa could even take a bite of food with the pigeons, the child ran toward him. Mustafa took off flying, skimming the heads of the crowd.

Just then an orange striped cat darted down the side street. Mustafa called out, “Ramazan, wait! Ramazan! Please!”

“Get away from me,” the cat hissed. “I don’t know you!”

Mustafa flew down the alley, seeing dogs, cafés and more people than he could count.

But suddenly, he only wanted to see Zehra’s smiling face.

TEA SHOP

Finally, he came out on the Istiklal Caddesi and found a red streetcar, sat on top and rode it all the way to the end.

Mustafa thought *If only I could get higher, I would be able to see my home. I'm sure of it!*

And higher he flew...

And higher...

Higher...

to the top of a beautiful tower. The view from Galata Tower was the most amazing thing he had ever seen.

A seagull called, “Merhaba, stranger! You new to these parts? It looks like you need a friend. I’m Ayhan. You want to come to Sultanahmet with me? There are some great things to see!”

Off they went, twisting and flying, laughing and wide-eyed, down to the bridge, past the fishermen, through the Spice Bazaar and out to the Ayasofya and the Blue Mosque.

They landed at the fountain and a young girl gently tossed pieces of simit towards them. She reminded Mustafa of Zehra in her beautiful green dress and suddenly he could eat no more.

“Why are you so sad, my dear friend?” Ayhan asked.

Lost, lost

Have you ever been lost?

In the unknown, far from home,

Roaming without a place to call your own?

Looking for the familiar,

Searching for what is right,

Feeling empty inside and having no where to hide?

"Ayhan, I feel lost."

"Well, let me help you," offered Ayhan. "The boats go everywhere — do you know where you live?"

Mustafa remembered Zehra practicing every night. He exclaimed, "Üsküdar! It's called Üsküdar!"

Down to the pier they flew with Ayhan calling out over the noise of the crowd. "I hear them yelling different places throughout the day. I've never actually had a home, so it wasn't important to me. But for you…."

Crowds of people were milling about headed in many directions. Just then a loudspeaker broke the silence, “Üsküdar! Üsküdar!”

“Hey there’s the boat! Good luck! Güle güle!”

Mustafa was tired as he perched on top of the ferry boat. It had been a long day and even though there were many adventures, he wanted to go home. Once they arrived at the pier, he started following a girl that looked like Zehra but it wasn’t her.

Mustafa perched in a tree, dejected, tired and hungry. He thought to himself, *I'm all alone in this big place. Help me find my home!*

Just then he saw the pet shop.

He speedily flew into the shop, circling and squawking with the other parrots. The kind shopkeeper gave Mustafa a perch with food and water. "Welcome, handsome green one! It is great to see you again! Make yourself at home. And speaking of home, where do you live now?"

"Üsküdar! Üsküdar!"

A smile crossed the shopkeeper's face. "Well, yes, but where? Do you know the street? You can trust me. I'll take care of you, just like I take care of all the others."

Mustafa thought for a moment, and then he said with boldness, "429 Lale Sokak, Üsküdar!"

"Well, right you are. You can wait here until closing time and then I will take you home. It's not everyday that such a beautiful bird returns to visit my shop!"

PET SHOP

LOST
MUSTAFA
Call: (0216) 428 - 3746
Address: 429 Lale Sokak Üsküdar

At 7:05 p.m., the shopkeeper delivered Mustafa to his home on Lale Sokak.

When they arrived, Mustafa noticed that Zehra had put up a sign next to the entrance door.

Mustafa had come home.

No one in Istanbul was happier that night than Zehra.

Unless, of course, you count parrots.

FOUND
MUSTAFA

Home is such a friendly place,

a needed space to be.

My heart is filled with beautiful flights,

the beautiful sights I've seen.

Now I have gone

Now I have flown

Once I was lost

But now I am found.

GLOSSARY

simplified pronunciations and definitions

Lale Sokak (LAH-leh SO-kahk) — Tulip Street

Üsküdar (OOS-koo-dar) — a large district on the Asian side of the Bosphorus in Istanbul

Taksim (TAk-sim) **Square** — an area on the European side of Istanbul from where the Istiklal Caddesi begins

İstiklal Caddesi (EES-teek-lal JAH-duh-see) — (Independence Avenue) is a pedestrian-oriented shopping street lined with cafés, boutiques, consulates, galleries and banks beginning at Taksim Square.

Sultanahmet (sool-tahn-AH-meht) — a neighborhood in the area of Fatih near the Golden Horn *(Haliç)* in Istanbul where you can find Ayasofya and the Blue Mosque, among other great sites

Galata (gah-LA-tah) **Tower** — Built in 1348, this tower (*Galata Kulesi)* was the tallest building in a Genoese area of Constantinople (now Istanbul) and was called the Tower of Christ

Merhaba (MARE-ha-ba) — Hello

Spice Bazaar — Egyptian (Spice) Bazaar *(Mısır Çarşısı)* is near the Galata Bridge in Istanbul. It is a shopping place for such things as spices, dried fruit, Turkish Delight (*lokum*), a variety of gold jewelry and many handmade souvenirs.

Ayasofya (eye-yah-so-FEE-yah) — The Church of the Divine Wisdom (*Hagia Sophia* in Greek) in Sultanahmet was built in 537 AD by Emperor Justinian. It was proclaimed a mosque by Mehmet the Conqueror in 1453 and in 1935, was turned into a museum by Mustafa Kemal "Atatürk," the founder of the Republic of Turkey.

Blue Mosque — The Mosque of Sultan Ahmet I (*Sultan Ahmet Camii*) was finished in 1617 and faces the north side of Ayasofya. It is referred to as the Blue Mosque because of the interior blue tiles in the upper galleries. Currently, it is a working mosque filled with many worshippers during the call to prayer and on Friday, the Muslim holy day.

Simit (si-MEET) — One of Turkey's national street snacks that is a circular bread topped with sesame seeds

Güle güle (gew-LEH gew-LEH) — Good-bye

47380745R00023

Made in the USA
Lexington, KY
04 December 2015